This book belongs to:

....

Peppa's
Treasury of Tales

M&S
KIDS

Marks and Spencer plc
PO Box 3339
Chester CH99 9QS

shop online
www.marksandspencer.com

978–0–241–27986–1
Printed in China

Contents

Daddy Pig's Office

Today, as a special treat,
Peppa and George are visiting
Daddy Pig's office.
"Daddy? Grunt. What do you
do at your office all day?"
asks Peppa.

"Lots of fun things!"
replies Daddy Pig.
"We're here!" he tells the
children as they arrive
at a very tall building.

"Hello!" Daddy Pig says into the intercom.
"Hello, Daddy Pig!" says a voice.
"Can I press the button?" Peppa asks.
"Ho! Ho! Of course, Peppa!" Daddy replies.

Beep!

"My office is at the top.
We have to go up in the lift,"
Daddy Pig tells the children.
"Can I press the button?
Snort!" asks Peppa excitedly.
"I think it's George's turn. Press
the top button please, George,"
says Daddy Pig.

The lift takes them to the top floor.
"Hello, everyone!" grunts Daddy Pig.
"Hello," say Mr Rabbit and Mrs Cat.
They work with Daddy Pig.

"I have two special visitors with me today – Peppa and George!" says Daddy Pig.

"Let's begin a tour!" suggests Daddy Pig.
"Mr Rabbit, can we start at your desk?"
"We certainly can!" replies Mr Rabbit.
"My job is all about numbers."

Grunt!

Hee! Hee!
Hee!

IN

"I take important pieces of paper and stamp
them with a rubber stamp," Mr Rabbit tells them.

"Wow!" gasp the children.
Peppa likes stamping paper.

"Ho! Ho! On with the tour! Next is
Mrs Cat's desk!" exclaims Daddy Pig.

"Hello, Peppa and George," says Mrs Cat.
"My job is all about drawing shapes on a computer."

"Can I try?" asks Peppa.

"I think it's George's turn," says Daddy Pig.

"Yes. It's your turn to work, George," says Peppa.

"Snort," agrees George.

Mrs Cat helps George make lots of blue triangles.

Grunt!

Grunt!

The printer spits sheets of paper everywhere!
"Hee! Hee!" George and Peppa think it's hilarious.
"Do you want to see my desk?" Daddy Pig asks.
"Yes please! Grunt!" says Peppa.

Daddy Pig's job
is very important.
"Do you use stamps
or a computer?"
asks Peppa.
"No," replies Daddy Pig.
"I use coloured pens!"
Peppa and George love
colouring pens.

"George is drawing a dinosaur. George always draws dinosaurs," says Peppa, bored. "Dine-saw! Grrr!" says George.

Ding-ding! The office clock has just chimed.
"My goodness! Five o'clock already!"
says Daddy Pig.
It is time for Peppa, George and
Daddy Pig to go home.

"You've been doing my job very well!"
snorts Daddy Pig.
"I like doing Mr Rabbit's job and I like
doing Mrs Cat's job, but I like doing your job
the best, Daddy," says Peppa.

$$x = \frac{-b \pm \sqrt{\Delta}}{2a}$$

Peppa and George have had
an excellent day at Daddy Pig's office.

George and the Noisy Baby

Peppa and George's family are
having a sleepover at Cousin
Chloe's house.

Mummy Pig and Daddy Pig are
looking forward to an early night.
They've had a long journey.

"Hello!" cries Cousin Chloe.
"Hello!" shouts Aunty Pig.
"Hello!" booms Uncle Pig.

Everyone makes a lot of noise in
Cousin Chloe's house.
They are a very noisy family.

"First, we'll put Baby Alexander to bed,"
says Aunty Pig.
"This is his bedroom."

Aunty Pig turns up
Baby Alexander's musical mobile.
"Alexander likes noise," she explains.
"It sends him to sleep."

Peppa and George are staying
in Cousin Chloe's bedroom.
They are very excited.
"Night, night!" snorts Peppa.

Soon everyone is tucked
up in their beds, asleep.

"Waaahh!"
Baby Alexander is awake. Everyone is awake.
Uncle Pig tries vacuuming.

Vroom! Vroom!

Aunty Pig tries playing the trumpet.
"Noise is the best way to get Baby Alexander
to sleep," she says.

Daddy Pig has a quieter idea to try.

"When George was a baby we used to put him in his pram and wheel him round the house," he says. "That always sent him to sleep."

Daddy Pig pushes Baby Alexander in his pram. He only has to go round the house fifty times.

"Good!" he puffs at last. "Baby Alexander is asleep."

Daddy Pig and Baby Alexander are ready to come inside. Aunty Pig switches the alarm back on.

Yawn!

"George!" cries Daddy Pig.
"What are you doing up?"
"Yawn!" yawns George. "Noisy!"

Snuffle
Snuffle

Daddy Pig takes George and Baby Alexander back up to bed. He is about to turn the light off when . . .

"Waaahhhh!"

"Uh oh!" gasps George.
Baby Alexander is awake again. It is very noisy.

Daddy Pig decides to drive Baby Alexander around in the car. "Don't forget to turn off the alarm!" shouts Aunty Pig.

Daddy Pig forgets to
turn off the alarm.
The noisy house wakes everyone
up. Miss Rabbit zooms across in
her rescue helicopter.

"Is everyone all right down there?"
yells Miss Rabbit.
"Yes, thank you!" bellows Uncle Pig.

The alarm has worked.
Baby Alexander is fast asleep.
"And it's all down to my noisy daddy!" giggles Peppa.

Peppa Goes Boating

Peppa and her family have come to the lake to go boating.

"Boats! Boats! Get your boats here!"
calls Miss Rabbit.

"I've got canoes,"
says Miss Rabbit.
"Hmm . . ." says Daddy
Pig. "Paddling a canoe
is hard work."

"I've got sailing boats," says Miss Rabbit.
Daddy Pig isn't sure. Sailing a sailing boat
is a bit tricky.

"The pedalos look nice
and relaxing," smiles
Mummy Pig.
"Yes!" agrees Daddy Pig.
"They've got a big paddle
wheel to make them go."

2

Daddy Pig, Mummy Pig, Peppa and George all climb on to a pedalo. "You have to pedal," Miss Rabbit tells them. "Enjoy your boat trip!" "Off we go!" shouts Daddy Pig. Peppa and George giggle. It's like a bicycle on the water!

Splish! Splosh!

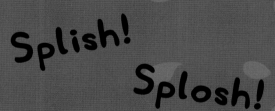

Emily Elephant
and her family arrive.
"Hello Miss Rabbit,"
says Mr Elephant. "We'd
like a canoe please!"

"Certainly!" says Miss Rabbit.

"Ahoy there, Miss Rabbit!"
It's Danny Dog and his dad,
Captain Dog! They want to go
out in a sailing boat.

"Aye, aye, Captain. I mean,
Dad!" says Danny Dog.

"We're sailing!" shouts Danny.
"We're canoeing!" shouts Emily.
"We're pedalling!" shouts Peppa.

Hee! Hee!

Poor Daddy Pig. Pedalling a pedalo
is a lot harder than it looks.

It is time to stop for lunch.
Mummy Pig passes around the sandwiches.
"Here's some bread for you,
Mrs Duck," grins Peppa.
Mrs Duck likes picnics!

Quack!

Quack!

Everyone likes picnics!

Miss Rabbit
rings her bell.

Ding!
Dong!

"Come in, boats one, two
and three," she calls.
"Your time is up!"

"One, two and three?" says Peppa. "That's us!"

"Let's see who can get back first,"
says Mummy Pig. "We'll have a race."

1

Everyone goes as fast as they can.
"I'm not sure I can pedal much
faster!" puffs Daddy Pig.
Captain Dog is lucky.
His boat has an engine.

2

3

55RXi

"We win!" cries Danny. Captain Dog cheers.
"I'm not a sailor any more," he says,
"but I do love boating on the lake!"

"Yes," says Peppa, "we all love boating on the lake!"

Hooray!

1

2

Peppa Goes Skiing

It is a lovely snowy day and Peppa's family are going skiing. First, they have to take a ski lift all the way to the top of Snowy Mountain.
"Oh . . . that looks a bit high," says Daddy Pig.
Daddy Pig does not like heights.

Everyone gets
on the ski lift.
"This is fun!"
calls Peppa,
and she sings
a little song.

Hee! Hee!
Hee!

"In the air! In a chair!
Snow is falling everywhere!"

Clunk!

Clank!

Daddy Pig does not think it is fun.
He does not like the way
the ski lift clunks and clanks.

At the top of
Snowy Mountain,
Daddy Pig falls out
of his chair and
into the snow!

"Are you all right,
Daddy?" cries Peppa.

"Ho! Ho! Yes, Peppa," says Daddy Pig. "Let's get you to your ski lesson."

Whoosh!

Madame Gazelle starts the ski lesson. Peppa, George and all their friends learn how to start and stop.

"Wheeee! Skiing is fun!" cries Peppa, as they go down the baby slope.

"Can we see *you* ski now,
Madame Gazelle?" asks Peppa.

"Oh, I don't know . . ."
replies Madame Gazelle.
"Please!" everyone cries.
"Very well," says Madame Gazelle.

Voila! Madame Gazelle does a magnificent ski jump.

Everyone claps and cheers.

"That was amazing!" says Peppa.
"Thank you," says Madame Gazelle.
"I was the world champion at
skiing and I won this cup!"
"Ooooh," everyone says.

"Which mummy or daddy would
like a go?" asks Madame Gazelle.
"I will!" says Mummy Pig.
"Where does this path lead?"
"Down the mountain!"
cries Madame Gazelle.

"Help! Where are the brakes?"
shouts Mummy Pig.

"She can't stop!" cries Daddy Pig.
"Let's catch up with her in the coach!"

Mummy Pig skis down the mountain,
along the road and past the shops!
"Eeeeeeeeee! Stand back!" cries Mummy Pig.
She even does a loop the loop at top speed!

Finally, everyone catches up with Mummy Pig.
She has crashed straight into a snowdrift!
"Snort! You're a walking, talking
snowman, Mummy!" laughs Peppa.

Snort!

"I have never seen such amazing skiing," says
Madame Gazelle. "This cup belongs to you now!"

Everyone cheers as Madame Gazelle presents
Mummy Pig with her world champion cup.
"Hooray!" says Peppa. "My mummy is a
skiing champion!"

Peppa Plays Basketball

It is a lovely sunny day.
Peppa and her friends
are in the playground.

Oooh!

"Children," says Madame Gazelle.
"Today we have a special person coming
to teach you basketball."

Oooh!

Daddy Pig walks into
the playground.
"Hello, everyone!"

"Daddy!" snorts Peppa.
"It isn't home time yet! We've got
a special teacher coming."
"That's me!" says Daddy Pig.

"I'm the coach," explains Daddy Pig.
A basketball teacher is called a coach.
Daddy Pig spins the ball on his finger.
"That's clever, Daddy!"
"Peppa," says Daddy Pig. "Call me Coach."

Daddy Coach blows his whistle.
"In basketball, you bounce the ball with
your hands," he says. "Everyone try!"

The children practise
bouncing the ball up and
down the playground.

"Throw the ball through the hoop!"
shouts Daddy Coach.

Oops! George throws the ball the wrong way.
He still needs a bit more training!

Daddy Coach decides it is
time to play a game.
"Split into two teams," he says.
The girls are in one team and the
boys are in the other.

"It's not fair," says Pedro Pony.
"We've got little ones on our team."
"Don't worry," says Danny Dog.
"The boys' team will still win."

The game starts.
Emily catches the ball with her trunk.
She is very good at reaching up high
with her trunk.

"That's not fair!" says Peppa.
"Shh!" whispers Suzy Sheep. "She's on our side!"
"Oh yes, it is fair," decides Peppa.

"We want Emily in our team!"
shouts Pedro Pony.
"No arguing," says Daddy Coach.
"You can all be on the same team."

The children get into one big team.
"But who will we play?" asks Peppa.
"Erm," says Daddy Coach. "Well . . ."

The parents arrive to take the children home.
"I know!" snorts Daddy Coach. "You can play
the grown-ups."
"But they're bigger than us!" cries Danny Dog.

"Ah," nods Daddy Coach,
"but you've been taught
basketball by Daddy Coach!"

"Yes!" calls Peppa. "Let's play!"
"All right!" shout the grown-ups.

George tackles Mr Elephant,
then passes to Zoe Zebra. Zoe passes
to Richard Rabbit.

Yippee!

Richard passes the ball to Peppa . . .
who throws it through the hoop!

Boing!

The final whistle blows.
The basketball game is over.

Everybody cheers. The children's
team have won!

Hooray!

Snort!

"And it's all thanks to Daddy Coach!"
says Peppa.

Woof!

George's New Dinosaur

George's favourite toy is Mr Dinosaur.
George likes bouncing Mr Dinosaur in the garden,
playing with him at bath time, and he loves going
to sleep with Mr Dinosaur beside him.

At bedtime Peppa says, "George, I think
Mr Dinosaur is broken!"

Mummy and Daddy Pig come in to
see why George is crying.
"Waaaaaaah!" cries George.
George is very upset.

"Poor George," says Daddy Pig.
"Maybe it's time you got
a new dinosaur."

The next day, Peppa, George, Mummy and Daddy Pig visit Mr Fox's shop. "I'm sure we'll find a lovely dinosaur here, George!" says Mummy Pig. "Look, George!" says Daddy Pig pointing to the shop window. "There's a big one!" "Oooh, dine-saw!" says George.

"Good morning!" beams Mr Fox. "Can I help you?"
"We'd like to buy the dinosaur in the window,
please," says Daddy Pig.
"Good choice!" says Mr Fox. "This is Dino-Roar.
He walks, he talks and he sings!"
"Wow!" says everyone.
"Dino-ROAR!" says George excitedly.
"We'll take it!" says Daddy Pig.

George is playing with Dino-Roar in the garden.
Dino-Roar sings,
"Dino-Roar, Dino-Roar!
Listen to Dino-Roar! Roooooaaaaaaaar!"
"Careful, George," says Daddy Pig. "Don't play
too roughly because Dino-Roar will get broken."

George wants to play with Dino-Roar
in the bath.

SPLASH,
SPLASH,

SPLASH!

"Dino-ROAR!" says George.
But Mummy Pig says, "George, if you get
Dino-Roar wet he'll stop working."

Peppa and George are asleep in bed. But suddenly Dino-Roar comes to life!

"ROAR! Dino-Roar, Dino-Roar!"

"George!" says Peppa. "Dino-Roar has woken me up!"

"Maybe Dino-Roar should sleep somewhere else," says Daddy Pig, taking Dino-Roar away.

George is feeling sad. He cannot play with Dino-Roar in the garden, or the bath or even in bed.

"Never mind, George," says Mummy Pig brightly.
"Dino-Roar can still roar."
"Dino-Roar! Li . . . sten to Dino-Roo . . . aarr."
Dino-Roar stops walking and talking completely.

"I think the batteries must have run out," says Mummy Pig.

"Already? How many are there?" grumbles Daddy Pig, as batteries pour out of Dino-Roar. "Hundreds and thousands!" cries Peppa, as she picks them up.

Peppa spots something green under a bush.
"What's this?" says Peppa. "Is it a trumpet?"
"You've found Mr Dinosaur's tail," says Mummy Pig.
"Now Daddy Pig can mend him."
"He might be a bit difficult to mend,"
says Daddy Pig doubtfully.

But the tail slips perfectly into place.
Daddy Pig has mended Mr Dinosaur.
"Ho ho ho," chuckles Daddy Pig.
"Hello, Mr Dinosaur," says Peppa.
"Grrrrr!" replies George.

"Hee! Hee!" everybody laughs.
Mr Dinosaur is George's favourite
toy in the whole world!

CLICK!

Miss Rabbit's
Day Off

Peppa, George and Suzy Sheep have had
a sleepover at Rebecca Rabbit's house.

Crunch!

Munch!

Crunch!

"It's fun having carrots for breakfast!" laughs Peppa.
"I could eat carrots all day!" agrees Daddy Rabbit.

Mummy Rabbit's sister, Miss Rabbit,
pops in to say hello.

"I can't stop long," she says. "I've got lots of work to do. I'm working at the supermarket, selling ice creams and driving the bus!"

Miss Rabbit trips over
one of Richard's toys.
Her ankle is hurt.

"You must stay here and get better," decides Mummy Rabbit. "I'll do your work for you."

Oww!

Mummy Rabbit puts Rebecca and her
friends in charge of looking after Miss Rabbit.

Luckily, Suzy Sheep has
her nurse's outfit with her.

"Don't worry," she says.
"I am only a pretend nurse!"

Mummy Rabbit goes straight to the supermarket. "Miss Rabbit is ill," she tells everyone. "I'll be doing her job today."

Peppa phones Miss Rabbit's ice cream stall.
Daddy Pig answers.
"Miss Rabbit is ill. You've got to sell the
ice cream today!"

"Ho, ho!" snorts Daddy Pig. "I'm an expert at ice cream!"
He gets to work.

Selling ice cream is quite hard.
Soon the ice cream begins to melt.

The ice cream is all runny.
"Ice cream soup, anyone?" asks Daddy Pig.

Peppa phones Grandad Dog.
"Miss Rabbit is very ill. Can you
drive her bus today, please?"

Grandad Dog gets to work, but driving a bus is quite hard. It is even harder when you have cars to fix, too.

Back at Rebecca Rabbit's house,
Miss Rabbit is feeling better.
"Can I get up now?" she asks.

Suzy Sheep shakes her head.
"No! You must lie very still . . . but
please keep breathing."

"It's not easy doing all your jobs," says
Mummy Rabbit at the end of the day.

"It's not easy sitting down all day!" says Miss Rabbit.
She will definitely be back at work tomorrow!

Mr Bull in a China Shop

It's a lovely day. Daddy Pig is taking
everyone out for a drive.
"Stop!" shouts Mr Bull.
"We're digging up the road."

"Digger!" shouts George.
George likes diggers.

Chug!
Chug!

Daddy Pig waits at the red light.
"Will the digging take long?"
asks Mummy Pig.

"It will take as long as it takes!" shouts Mr Bull.
Mr Bull walks off. It is time for his tea break.

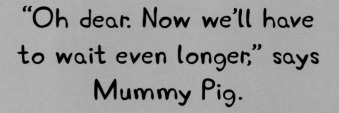

"Oh dear. Now we'll have to wait even longer," says Mummy Pig.

"Why don't you join us?" booms Mr Bull.
"Thank you!" Mummy Pig smiles.
Everybody sits down.
Mr Bull pours out the tea.

"That's a nice teapot," says Peppa. "Yes!" snorts Mr Bull. "It's made of delicate china."

Mr Bull puts the teapot
down on the table too hard.
"Oh no," he yells. "I've broken it!"

Mr Bull doesn't know his own strength sometimes. He is very sad.

"Miss Rabbit has a china shop," says Mummy Pig. "She could mend the teapot."

"Good idea!" shouts Mr Bull.
"We'll go right now!"

Mr Bull drives all the way to the china shop.
Miss Rabbit is hard at work.
"Moo!" bellows Mr Bull.

Miss Rabbit looks up.
"Aaagh!" she wails. "A bull in a china shop!"

"I have broken my china teapot!" cries Mr Bull.
Miss Rabbit takes a look at the teapot.

"Hmm," she frowns.
"That's very broken . . . but I think I can fix it."

Miss Rabbit gets out some glue.
Fixing a teapot is like doing a jigsaw puzzle.
"The pieces fit together," says Peppa.
"There's just one funny-shaped bit left,"
says Miss Rabbit.

Peppa giggles. Miss Rabbit has found the handle!

Miss Rabbit gives the teapot back to Mr Bull. "It's as good as new!" he bellows. "Thank you."

Ho! Ho!

"Be careful not to smash it again,"
says Miss Rabbit.
"I am very good at smashing things!"
agrees Mr Bull.

Outside the china shop there is a hole in
the road. "Look, boss," says Mr Labrador.

Mr Bull makes up his mind. Miss Rabbit
can't have a hole outside her shop!

"You fixed my teapot," shouts Mr Bull.
"I'll fix your road!"
"How are you going to mend the hole?" wonders Peppa

Mr Bull grins.
"We'll dig up the road!"
Mr Bull likes digging up the road!

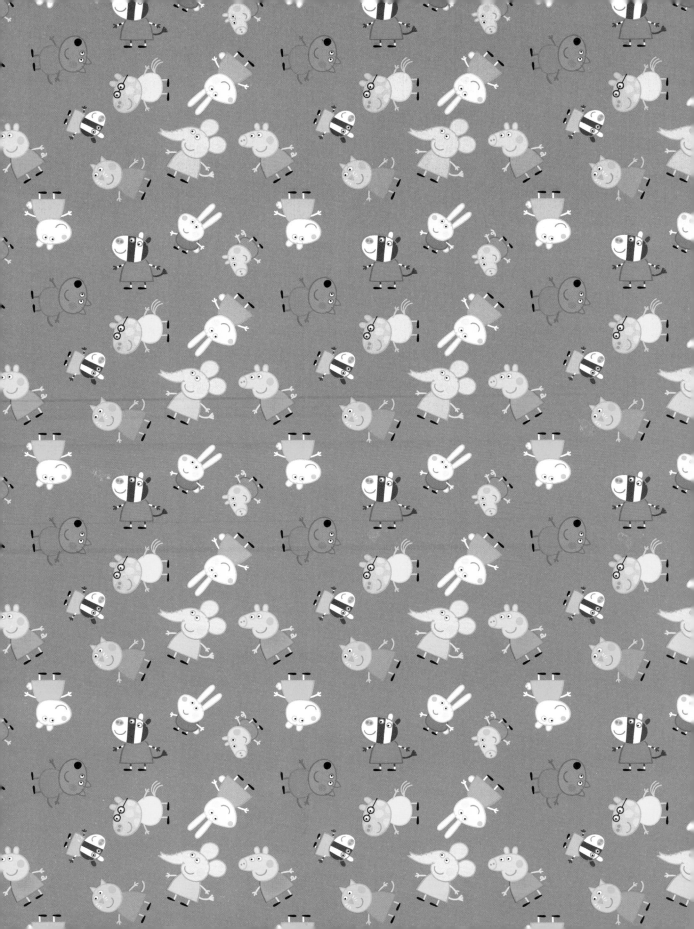